The Key
La Clé

David Gordon Stanley

Illustrated by Dimitra Megkou

Aide translation Lorelei Surdu

The Key

DAVID GORDON STANLEY

WORKBOOK PRESS LLC
187 E Warm Springs Rd
Suite B285 Las Vegas NV 89119 USA

Website: https://workbookpress.com/
Hotline: 1-888-818-4856
Email: admin@workbookpress.com

Ordering Information:
Quantity sales. Special discounts are available on quantity purchases by corporations, associations, and others. For details, contact the publisher at the address above.

ISBN-13: 978-1-963718-71-3 Paperback Version
         978-1-963718-72-0 Digital Version

PUB. DATE: 06.30.2024

English: Magic moments
        French: Moments magic
                Italian: Magici momenti
                        Romanian: Momente magice
                                Spanish: Momentos mágicos

Contents

Leitmotif 1. Language pages:

Key Note pages - Leitmotif 2.

Language pages:

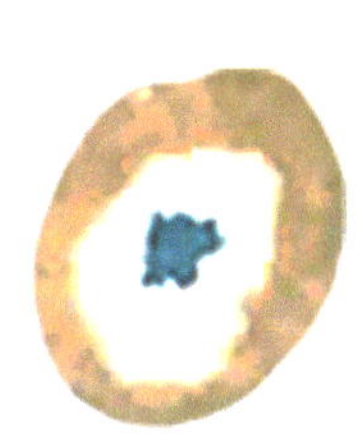

With love to my daughter Linda

Translations dedicated to Lorelei's daughter Simona
From the book's illustrator - To my beloved niece Konstania
My heart felt thanks to all who have contributed in making this book a success!

It was a beautiful summer's day; the birds were singing in the trees and the air was refreshing. I was walking through town and took a shortcut through the cemetery. Halfway I saw a small silver box on the path. I looked at it for a moment thinking "that's not yours, don't touch it."

French: C'était une belle journée d'été, les oiseaux chantaient dans les arbres et l'air était frais. Alors que j'étais en train de marcher dans la ville, j'ai pris un raccourci pour atteindre le cimetière.

A mi-chemin j'ai vu une petite boîte argentée sur ma voie. Je l'ai regardée pendant un bon moment en pensant "ce n'est pas la tienne, ne la touche pas."

Italian: E stato una volta una bella giornata festiva, gli ucceli cantavano e l'aria era pulita. Io stavo camminando nella città e ho preso una scorciatoia al cimitero. A metà strada, ho visto una piccola scatola d'argento sulla mia strada. L'ho guardata per un po' e ho pensato "questo non è tuo, non devi toccare."

Romanian: A fost o data o zi frumoasa de vara, in care pasarile cantau, in copaci si aerul era curat. Eu mergeam prin oras si am luat-o pe o scurtatura catre cimitir.

La jumatatea drumului, am vazut o cutie mica de argint in calea mea. M-am uitat o vreme la ea si m-am gandit "asta nu este a ta, nu o atinge."

Spainish: Era un hermoso día de verano, los pájaros cantaban en los árboles y el aire era refrescante. Estaba caminando por la ciudad y tomé un atajo por el cementerio.

A mitad de camino vi una pequeña caja plateada en el camino. Lo miré por un momento pensando "eso no es tuyo, no lo toques".

English: space for the language or creative text of your choice.

However, all the same, my curiosity won, I picked it up and opened it. Inside was a door key that looked like mine.

French: Cependant, ma curiosité gagna, j'ai l'ai ramassée et l'ai ouverte. A l'intérieur il y avait une clé qui ressemblait à la mienne.

Italian: Tuttavia, la mia curiosità ha avuto la meglio su di me, ne ho preso e l'ho aperto. Dentro c'era una chiave che sembrava il mio.

Romanian: Cu toate astea, insa curiozitatea mea m-a invins, am luat-o si am deschis-o. Inauntru era o cheie de la o usa care arata la fel ca cheia mea.

Spanish: Sin embargo, de todos modos, ganó mi curiosidad, lo recogí y lo abrí. Dentro había una llave de puerta que se parecía a la mía.

So, I decided to keep it and put it in my pocket, then I continued my journey through town.

I justified my actions by thinking that eventually, I could always return it to lost and found or to the local library.

French: Alors, j'ai décidé de la garder et de la mettre dans ma poche, puis j'ai continué mon voyage à dans la ville. J'ai justifié mes gestes en pensant qu'éventuellement, je pourrais toujours le déposer aux objets trouvés ou à la bibliothèque locale.

Italian: Così, ho deciso di tenerlo e metterlo in tasca, poi ho continuato il mio viaggio attraverso la città. Ho giustificato le mie azioni pensando che alla fine avrei sempre potuto restituirlo a oggetti smarriti o alla biblioteca locale.

Romanian: Asa ca am decis sa o pastrez si sa o pun in buzunarul meu, apoi am continuat calatoria prin oras. M-am gandit in sinea mea ca pot sa o aduc la lucruri gasite sau la biblioteca locala.

Spanish: Así que decidí quedármelo y ponerlo en mi bolsillo, luego continué mi viaje por la ciudad. Justifiqué mis acciones pensando que eventualmente siempre podría devolverlo a objetos perdidos oa la biblioteca local.

Italiano: spazio alla lingua o al testo creativo di tua scelta.

When I got home, I had completely forgotten about the key until I got to the door and the box started ringing in my pocket. In amazement, I pulled the box out of my pocket and opened it. The key slipped easily into the lock and to my surprise I opened the door. I put the box with the key in my jacket pocket.

French: Quand je suis rentré à la maison, j'avais complètement oublié la clé jusqu'à ce que j'arrive à la porte et la boîte a commencé à sonner dans ma poche. Stupéfait, j'ai sorti la boîte de ma poche et je l'ai ouverte. La clé glissa facilement dans la serrure et à ma surprise j'ai ouvert la porte. J'ai rangé la boîte avec la clé dans la poche de ma veste.

Italian: Quando sono tornato a casa mi ero completamente dimenticato della chiave finché non sono arrivato alla porta e la scatola ha iniziato a suonare nella mia tasca. Con stupore, ho tirato fuori la scatola dalla tasca e l'ho aperta. La chiave è scivolata facilmente nella serratura e con mia sorpresa ho aperto la porta. Misi la scatola con la chiave nella tasca della giacca.

Romanian: Cand am ajuns acasa am uitat tot de cheie, pana cand am ajuns la usa si cutia a inceput sa suna in buzunarul meu. Fascinat, am scos cutia din buzunar si am deschis-o.

Cheia a alunecat cu usurinta in broasca si spre surprinderea mea, a deschis usa. Am pus cutia cu cheia in buzunarul de la jacheta mea.

Spanish: Cuando llegué a casa me había olvidado por completo de la llave hasta que llegué a la puerta y la caja empezó a sonar en mi bolsillo. Con asombro, saqué la caja de mi bolsillo y la abrí.

La llave se deslizó fácilmente en la cerradura y para mi sorpresa abrí la puerta. Puse la caja con la llave en el bolsillo de mi chaqueta.

Română: Spațiu pentru limba sau textul creativ la alegere.

I had my lunch with two glasses of red wine and started thinking, then as usual I took a little nap.

French: J'ai pris mon déjeuner avec deux verres de vin rouge et j'ai commencé à réfléchir, puis comme d'habitude, j'ai fait une petite sieste.

Italian: Ho pranzato con due bicchieri di vino rosso e ho iniziato a pensare, poi come al solito ho fatto un sonnellino.

Romanian: Am servit pranzul si doua pahare cu vin rosu apoi am inceput sa ma gandesc, apoi ca de obicei am facut siesta.

Spanish: Comí mi almuerzo con dos copas de vino tinto y comencé a pensar, luego, como de costumbre, tomé una pequeña siesta.

Español: espacio para el idioma o texto creativo de su elección.

After doing the dishes, I wanted to take a drive. I approached the garage door which was obviously locked. Suddenly the box with the key rang. Again, I took out the key and slipped it into the lock. Incredibly, it opened, in short, I put the box in my pocket and approaching my car the box rang again. Surprised I tried the key in the door of the car and it opened it.

French: Après avoir fait la vaisselle, j'ai eu envie de faire un tour en voiture. Je m'approchai de la porte du garage qui était évidemment fermée à clé. Tout à coup, la boîte avec la clé sonna. A nouveau, j'ai sorti la clé et l'ai glissée dans la serrure. C'était incroyable, pour faire court, cela s'est ouvert. J'ai mis la boite dans ma poche et je me suis approché de ma voiture quand la clé a recommencé à sonner. Surpris, j'ai essayé la clef dans la portière de ma voiture et elle s'est ouverte.

Italian: Dopo aver lavato i piatti, volevo fare un giro. Mi sono avvicinato alla porta del garage che era ovviamente chiusa a chiave. All'improvviso la scatola con il portachiavi. Ancora una volta, tirai fuori la chiave e la infilai nella serratura. Incredibilmente si aprì, insomma mi misi la scatola in tasca e avvicinandomi alla macchina la scatola corse di nuovo. Sorpreso ho provato la chiave nella portiera della macchina e l'ha aperta.

Romanian: Dupa ce am spalat vasele, am vrut sa conduc masina. M-am indreptat catre usa garajului care era bineinteles incuiata. Deodata cutia cu cheia a sunat. Iarasi, am scos cheia si am bagat-o in broasca. A fost incredibil, s-a deschis, am pus cutia in buzunarul meu si apropiindu-ma de masina, cutia a sunat din nou. Surprins am incercat cheia in broasca din usa masinii si s-a deschis.

Spanish: Después de lavar los platos, quería dar una vuelta. Me acerqué a la puerta del garaje que obviamente estaba cerrada. De repente la caja con el llavero. Una vez más, saqué la llave y la deslicé en la cerradura.   Increíblemente se abrió, en fin, puse la caja en mi bolsillo y al acercarme a mi carro la caja volvió a correr. Sorprendido probé la llave en la puerta del auto y lo abrió.

The same key started the engine. So, I drove to the petrol station which was closed that Sunday. However, as I had understood the use of the key, I approached the fuel pump that was locked, and to my satisfaction the silver box began to ring.

French: La même clé a démarré le moteur. J'ai donc conduit jusqu'à la station-service qui était fermée ce dimanche-là. Cependant, comme j'avais compris l'usage de la clé je me suis approché de la pompe à essence, qui était fermée à clé, et pour ma satisfaction, la boite argentée a commencé à sonner.

Italian: La stessa chiave ha avviato il motore. Così sono andato al distributore di benzina che quella domenica era chiuso. Tuttavia, siccome avevo capito l'uso della chiave mi sono avvicinato alla pompa del carburante che era chiusa a chiave, e per la mia soddisfazione la scatola d'argento ha cominciato a suonare.

Spanish: La misma llave arrancó el motor. Así que conduje hasta la gasolinera que estaba cerrada ese domingo. Sin embargo, como había entendido el uso de la llave, me acerqué a la bomba de combustible que estaba bloqueada y, para mi satisfacción, la caja plateada comenzó a sonar.

Romanian: Aceeasi cheie a pornit motorul, asa ca am condus pana la statia de carburant care era inchisa in acea duminica. Cu toate acestea, cum am inteles la ce folosea cheia, m-am apropiat de pompa care era inchisa, si spre satisfactia mea, cutia de argint a inceput sa sune.

Russian - Русский: пространство для языка или творческого текста по вашему выбору.

Of course, it worked wonderfully to unlock the pump. I filled up and decided to go to the bank. In front of the bank door, my box rang. With a smile, I slipped the key into the lock.

French: Bien sûr, cela a fonctionné merveilleusement pour déverrouiller la pompe. J'ai fait le plein et j'ai décidé d'aller à la banque. Devant la porte de la banque, ma boîte a sonné. Avec un sourire, j'ai glissé la clé dans la serrure.

Italian: Certo, ha funzionato meravigliosamente per sbloccare la pompa. Ho fatto il pieno e ho deciso di andare in banca. Davanti alla porta della banca, il mio box squillò. Con un sorriso, ho infilato la chiave nella serratura.

Romanian: Bineanteles, deblocarea pompei a decurs minunat. Am facut plinul si am decis sa merg la banca. In fata usii de la banca, cutia mea a sunat. Cu un zambet, am bagat cheia in incuietoare. În fața ușii băncii, mi-a sunat cutia. Cu un zâmbet, am strecurat cheia în broască.

Spanish: Por supuesto, funcionó maravillosamente para desbloquear la bomba. Me llené y decidí ir al banco. Frente a la puerta del banco sonó mi caja. Con una sonrisa, deslicé la llave en la cerradura.

Japonais: 日本語:選択した言語またはクリエイティブテキストのためのスペース。

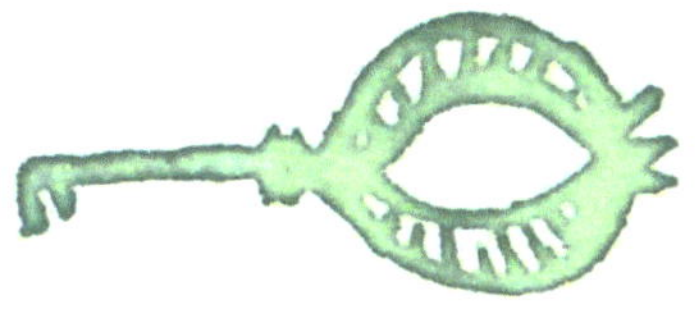

Then I stopped. A sudden realisation. On the other side of the door was the money, but also the silent alarms, total security! As in a flash I put the key and the box in my pocket. All this did not happen by chance, so to understand more, I returned to the cemetery, strangely it was locked. I approached the gate of the cemetery and the box rang very loudly.

French: Puis je me suis arrêté. Une prise de conscience soudaine. De l'autre côté de la porte se trouvait l'argent, mais aussi les alarmes silencieuses, la sécurité totale! Comme dans un flash j'ai rangé la clé et la boîte dans ma poche. Tout ça n'est pas arrivé par hasard, alors pour comprendre davantage, je suis retourné au cimetière, étrangement, il était fermé à clé. Je m'approchai de la porte du cimetière et la boîte sonna très fort.

Italian: Poi ho smesso. Una presa di coscienza improvvisa. Dall'altra parte della porta c'erano i soldi, ma anche gli allarmi silenziosi, la sicurezza totale! Come in un lampo metto in tasca la chiave e la scatola. Tutto ciò non è avvenuto per caso, quindi per capirci di più sono tornata al cimitero, stranamente era chiuso a chiave. Mi sono avvicinato al cancello del cimitero e la cassetta ha suonato molto forte.

Romanian: Dupa care, m-am oprit. Mi-am dat seama dintr-o data. De cealaltă parte a ușii erau banii, dar și alarmele silentioase, securitate totală! Ca într-o clipită am pus cheia și cutia în buzunar. Toate astea nu s-au petrecut din noroc, asa ca pentru a intelege mai bine, m-am intors la cimitir, in mod ciudat era incuiat. M-am apropiat de poarta cimitirului si cutia a sunat foarte tare.

Spanish: Entonces me detuve. Una realización repentina. Al otro lado de la puerta estaba el dinero, pero también las alarmas silenciosas, ¡seguridad total! Como en un relámpago, guardé la llave y la caja en el bolsillo. Todo esto no sucedió por casualidad, así que para entender más, regresé al cementerio, extrañamente estaba cerrado. Me acerqué a la puerta del cementerio y la caja sonó muy fuerte.

Svenska: Utrymme för det språk eller den kreativa text du väljer.

To my surprise, the gate was opened by a man who must have been about the age of my great-great-grandfather. He greeted me and told me he was there to escort me to my grave. Intrigued, I followed him to the middle of the cemetery and we stopped in front of an old door, unfortunately my silver box rang.

French: À ma grande surprise, la porte a été ouverte par un homme qui devait avoir à peu près l'âge de mon arrière-arrière-grand-père. Il m'a saluée et m'a dit qu'il était là pour m'escorter à ma tombe. Intrigué, je l'ai suivi jusqu'au milieu du cimetière et nous nous sommes arrêté devant une vieille porte, malheureusement ma boîte argentée a sonné.

Italian: Con mia grande sorpresa, il cancello è stato aperto da un uomo che doveva avere all'incirca l'età del mio bis-bisnonno. Mi salutò e mi disse che era lì per accompagnarmi alla tomba. Incuriosito l'ho seguito fino al centro del cimitero e ci siamo fermati davanti ad una vecchia porta, purtroppo la mia cassetta d'argento ha suonato.

Romanian: Spre surprinderea mea, poarta a fost deschisa de un barbat care era de varsta strabunicului meu. M-a salutat si mi-a spus ca era acolo ca sa ma conduca la mormantul meu. Intrigat, l-am urmat in mijlocul cimitirului si ne-am oprit in fata unei usi vechi, din pacate cutia mea de argint a sunat.

Spanish: Para mi sorpresa, la puerta fue abierta por un hombre que debía tener la edad de mi tatarabuelo. Me saludó y me dijo que estaba allí para acompañarme a mi tumba. Intrigado, lo seguí hasta el medio del cementerio y nos detuvimos frente a una puerta vieja, lamentablemente sonó mi caja de plata.

Chinese - 中文：为您选择的语言或创意文本留出空间。

 I started to feel bad; with a small tremor, I took the box out of my pocket. Desperate and unbalanced, I threw the box in the middle of the path and it fell right where I found it.

French: J'ai commencé à me sentir mal, avec un petit tremblement, je sortis la boîte de ma poche. Désespéré et déséquilibré, j'ai jeté la boîte au milieu du chemin et elle est tombée là où je l'avais trouvée.

Italian: Ho iniziato a sentirmi male; con un piccolo tremito, tirai fuori la scatola dalla tasca. Disperato e sbilanciato, ho lanciato la scatola in mezzo al sentiero e sono caduto proprio dove l'avevo trovata.

Romanian: M-am simtit rau; cu un usor tremurat, am scos cutia din buzunar. Disperat si dezechilibrat, am aruncat cutia in mijlocul drumului si a cazut chiar acolo unde o gasisem.

Spanish: Empecé a sentirme mal; con un pequeño temblor, saqué la caja de mi bolsillo. Desesperado y desequilibrado, tiré la caja en medio del camino y caí justo donde la encontré.

At the same time, I quickly ran to my car, but it was locked. No problem I had the original key!
I took the real key out of my pocket and got into the car. Two seconds later I was on the main road going a hundred miles an hour.

French: En même temps, j'ai rapidement couru vers ma voiture, mais elle était verrouillée. Pas de problème, j'avais la clé d'origine! J'ai pris la vraie clé de ma poche et je suis montée dans la voiture. Deux secondes plus tard j'étais sur la route principale à cent à l'heure.

Italian: Allo stesso tempo, sono corso velocemente alla mia macchina, ma era chiusa a chiave. Nessun problema avevo la chiave originale! Tirai fuori dalla tasca la vera chiave e salii in macchina. Due secondi dopo ero sulla strada principale a cento all'ora.

Romanian: În acelasi moment, am alergat rapid catre masina mea, dar era incuiata. Nici o problema, aveam cheia veche. Am scos cheia adevărată din buzunar si am urcat în masină. Doua secunde mai tarziu eram pe strada principala conducant cu 100 de mile la ora.

Spanish: Al mismo tiempo, corrí rápidamente hacia mi auto, pero estaba cerrado. ¡No hay problema, tenía la llave original! Saqué la llave real de mi bolsillo y me subí al auto. Dos segundos después estaba en la carretera principal a cien millas por hora.

English: space for the language or creative text of your choice.

Unsurprisingly, a police car came out of nowhere and started chasing me. I regained my composure and stopped in front of the petrol station I had visited two hours earlier.

French: Sans surprise, une voiture de police est sortie de nulle part et a commencé à me poursuivre. J'ai retrouvé mon calme et me suis arrêté en face de la station-service que j'avais visitée deux heures plus tôt.

Italian: Non sorprende che una macchina della polizia sia spuntata dal nulla e abbia iniziato a inseguirmi. Ripresi la calma e mi fermai davanti al distributore di benzina che avevo visitato due ore prima.

Romanian: Fara surpriza, o masina de politie a venit de niciunde si a inceput sa ma urmareasca. Mi-am regasit echilibrul de sine si m-am oprit in fata statiei de carburant pe care o vizitasem cu doua ore inainte.

Spanish: Como era de esperar, un coche de policía salió de la nada y comenzó a perseguirme. Recuperé la compostura y me detuve frente a la gasolinera que había visitado dos horas antes.

Français: espace pour la langue ou le texte créatif de votre choix.

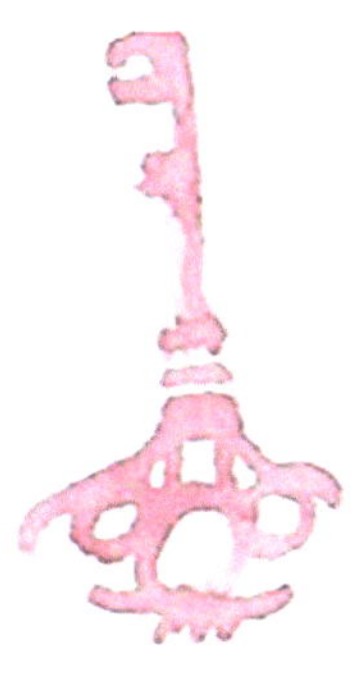

At this time there was a crowd around the pumps. As soon as I stopped the whole crowd fell silent and looked at me. Two policemen came out of the crowd and questioned me.

"Sir, would you please get out of the car?"

French: Il y avait à ce moment une foule autour des pompes. Dès que je suis arrêté toute la foule fit silence et me regarda. Deux policiers sortirent de la foule et m'interpellèrent.
« Monsieur, voulez-vous sortir de la voiture s'il vous plaît? »

Italian: In questo momento c'era una folla intorno alle pompe. Non appena mi sono fermato, tutta la folla è rimasta in silenzio e mi ha guardato. Due poliziotti sono usciti dalla folla e mi hanno interrogato. "Signore, potrebbe scendere dall'auto?"

Romanian: In acel moment, era o multime de oameni in jurul pompelor. De indata ce m-am oprit toata lumea a tacut si m-a privit. Doi politisti au iesit din multime si mi-au pus intrebari. "Domnule, puteti sa iesiti va rog din masina?"

Spanish: En este momento había una multitud alrededor de las bombas. Tan pronto como me detuve, toda la multitud se quedó en silencio y me miró. Dos policías salieron de la multitud y me interrogaron. "Señor, ¿podría salir del auto?"

Italiano: spazio alla lingua o al testo creativo di tua scelta.

"We saw the surveillance video and it was you who used the pump without paying, wasn't it?"
As I stammered, I said, "Yeah! Indeed, something weird happened to me!"
They listened to me then, "We believe you sir, would you follow us to the police station please?"

French: « On a vu la vidéo de surveillance et c'est bien vous qui vous êtes servi de l'essence sans payer, n'est pas? »

En balbutiant j'ai répondu « Ouais! En effet une chose bizarre m'est arrivé! »

Ils m'écoutèrent puis « On vous croît monsieur, voulez-vous nous suivre jusqu'au commissariat s'il vous plaît? »

Italian: "Abbiamo visto il video della sorveglianza e sei stato tu ad usare la pompa senza pagare, vero?" Mentre balbettavo dissi: "Sì! In effetti, mi è successo qualcosa di strano!

Poi mi hanno ascoltato: "Le crediamo signore, ci seguirebbe alla stazione di polizia per favore?"

Romanian: „Am văzut filmul de supraveghere și tu ai fost cel care ai folosit pompa fără să plătești, nu-i așa?" În timp ce mă bâlbâiam, am spus: „Da! Într-adevăr, mi s-a întâmplat ceva ciudat!" M-au ascultat si apoi mi-au raspuns : „Vă credem, domnule, vă rog să ne urmăriți până la secția de poliție?"

Spanish: "Vimos el video de vigilancia y fuiste tú quien usó la bomba sin pagar, ¿no?"
Mientras tartamudeaba dije: "¡Sí! De hecho, ¡algo extraño me pasó!"
Me escucharon entonces, "Le creemos señor, ¿nos sigue hasta la comisaría por favor?"

Approaching the police station my box started ringing. As if by magic the box had returned to its place!

French: En approchant du commissariat ma boîte a commencé à sonner. Comme par magie la boîte avait regagné sa place !

Italian: Avvicinandosi alla stazione di polizia la mia casella ha iniziato a suonare. Come per magia la scatola era tornata al suo posto!

Romanian: Apropiindu-mă de secția de poliție, caseta mea a început să sune. Ca prin magie, cutia se întorsese la locul ei!

Spanish: Al acercarme a la comisaría mi caja empezó a sonar. ¡Como por arte de magia la caja había vuelto a su sitio!

Español: espacio para el idioma o texto creativo de su elección.

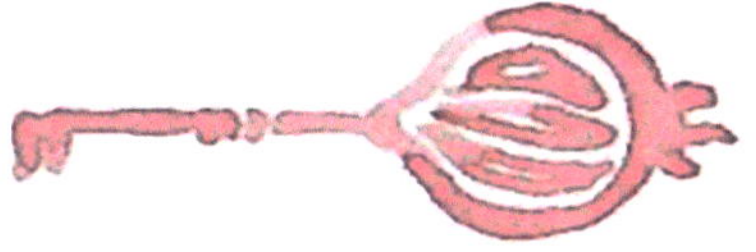

The police looked at me and with a nod let me open the locked door. Then they guided me to the chief's office. Behind the desk was a young woman in her mid-thirties with sparkling blue eyes and brown hair.

French: La police m'a regardé et d'un signe de tête m'a laissé ouvrir la porte verrouillée. Puis ils m'ont guidé jusqu'au bureau du chef. Derrière le bureau se trouvait une jeune femme d'environ trente ans avec des yeux bleus étincelants et les cheveux bruns.

Italian: La polizia mi ha guardato e con un cenno mi ha lasciato aprire la porta chiusa a chiave. Poi mi hanno guidato all'ufficio del capo. Dietro la scrivania c'era una giovane donna sui trentacinque anni con scintillanti occhi azzurri e capelli castani.

Romanian: Politia s-a uitat la mine si, cu un semn din cap, m-a lăsat să deschid usa încuiată. Apoi m-au condus la biroul sefului. În spatele biroului se afla o tânără de vreo treizeci de ani, cu ochi albastri strălucitori si păr castaniu.

Spanish: El policía me miró y con un movimiento de cabeza me dejó abrir la puerta cerrada. Luego me guiaron a la oficina del jefe. Detrás del escritorio había una mujer joven de treinta y tantos años con brillantes ojos azules y cabello castaño.

Deutsch: Platz für die sprache oder den kreativen text ihrer wahl.

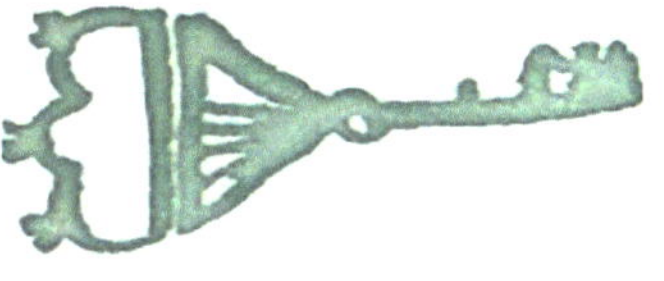

She ushered me to the side where there was a plush coffee area. There, the chief offered me a small coffee, a croissant and a small chocolate bar. She was very nice and explained to me that she knew well the history of the universal silver key and now it was my turn to have it.

French: Elle m'a conduit sur le côté où se trouvait un coin café somptueux. Là, la cheffe m'offre un petit café, un croissant et une petite barre de chocolat. Elle était très gentille et m'a expliqué qu'elle connaissait bien l'histoire de la clé d'argent universelle et que maintenant c'était à mon tour de l'avoir.

Italian: Mi ha accompagnato sul lato dove c'era un'elegante zona caffè. Lì, il capo mi ha offerto un piccolo caffè, un cornetto e una tavoletta di cioccolato. Lei è stata molto gentile e mi ha spiegato che conosceva bene la storia della chiave universale d'argent e ora toccava a me averla.

Romanian: Ea m-a condus într-o parte unde era o zonă de cafea de pluș. Acolo, șefa mi-a oferit o cafea mică, un croissant și un mic baton de ciocolată. A fost foarte drăguță și mi-a explicat că ea cunoaște bine istoria cheii universale de argint și acum a venit rândul meu să o am.

Spanish: Me condujo al lado donde había una lujosa área de café. Allí, el jefe me ofreció un pequeño café, un croissant y una pequeña barra de chocolate. Ella fue muy amable y me explicó que conocía bien la historia de la llave de plata universal y ahora me tocaba a mí tenerla.

Russian - Русский: пространство для языка или творческого текста по вашему выбору.

Obviously, the key had adopted me like all the others during the centuries, who had disappeared into nature. She explained to me that the old man I had met was actually a former judge. I was free to leave, but the next day I would have to pay the mechanic for the petrol, otherwise there would be legal proceedings. Her last words, in good humour, were "However, and above all, be careful with your key in the future and no nonsense!"

French: Évidemment la clé m'avait adopté comme tous les autres au cours des siècles, qui avaient disparu dans la nature. Elle m'a expliqué que le vieil homme que j'avais rencontré était en fait un ancien juge. J'étais libre de partir, mais le lendemain je devais payer l'essence au garagiste, sinon il y aurait des poursuites judiciaires. Ses derniers mots dans la bonne humeur étaient « Toutefois et surtout soyez prudent avec votre clé à l'avenir et pas de bêtises ! »

Italian: Ovviamente la chiave mi aveva adottato come tutti gli altri nel corso dei secoli, scomparsi nella natura. Mi ha spiegato che il vecchio che avevo incontrato era in realtà un ex giudice. Ero libero di partire, ma l'indomani avrei dovuto pagare la benzina al meccanico, altrimenti ci sarebbe stato il procedimento giudiziario. Le sue ultime parole, di buon umore, furono "Tuttavia, e soprattutto, stai attento con la tua chiave in futuro e niente sciocchezze!"

Romanian: Evident, cheia mă adoptase ca toți ceilalți de-a lungul secolelor, care dispăruseră în natură. Ea mi-a explicat că bătrânul pe care l-am întâlnit era de fapt un fost judecător. Eram liber să plec, dar a doua zi trebuia să-i plătesc mecanicului benzina, altfel s-ar fi procedat în justiție.
Ultimele ei cuvinte, de bună dispoziție, au fost „Totuși, și mai presus de toate, fii atent la cheia ta în viitor și fără prostii!"

Spanish: Evidentemente la llave me había adoptado como todos los demás durante los siglos, que habían desaparecido en la naturaleza. Me explicó que el anciano que había conocido era en realidad un ex juez. Era libre de irme, pero al día siguiente tendría que pagarle al mecánico la gasolina, de lo contrario habría procedimientos legales.
Sus últimas palabras, de buen humor, fueron "Sin embargo, y sobre todo, ¡cuidado con tu llave en el futuro y nada de tonterías!".

Japonais - 日本語:選択した言語またはクリエイティブテキストのためのスペース。

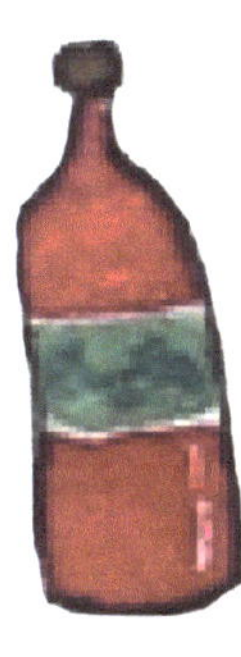

Epilogue

It was fifteen years later that, as a homeless person without a car and without a job, I went back to the pawn shop to pick up my key to go to the cemetery and open my grave...

But that's another story!

8/12/09

Épilogue

French: Quinze ans plus tard, en tant que S.D.F, sans voiture et sans emploi je suis retourné chez ma tante pour récupérer ma clé pour aller au cimetière et ouvrir ma tombe…

Mais ça c'est une autre histoire!

8/12/09

Epilogo

Italian: Sono passati quindici anni da quando, da senzatetto senza macchina e senza lavoro, sono tornato al banco dei pegni per ritirare la mia chiave per andare al cimitero e aprire la mia tomba...

Ma questa è un'altra storia!

8/12/09

Epilog

Romanian: Cincisprezece ani mai târziu, în calitate de persoană fără adăpost, fără mașină și fără loc de muncă, m-am întors la casa de amanet să-mi iau cheia pentru a merge la cimitir și a-mi deschide mormântul...

Dar asta e alta poveste!

8/12/09

Epílogo

Spanish: Fue quince años después que, como un vagabundo sin coche y sin trabajo, volví a la casa de empeño a recoger mi llave para ir al cementerio y abrir mi tumba...

¡Pero esa es otra historia!

8/12/09

Svenska: Utrymme för det språk eller den kreativa text du väljer.

Author's note.

I really enjoyed writing the story "The key." In fact, I was inspired by the story 'Le Veston' by Dino Buzzati. When I started writing it, I was anxious, nervous, hesitant, and felt a real lack of confidence.

French: Note d'Auteur.
J'ai vraiment aimé écrire l'histoire « la clé ». En fait, j'ai été inspiré par l'histoire « Le Veston » de Dino Buzzati. Quand j'ai commencé à l'écrire, j'étais anxieuse, nerveuse, hésitante et je ressentais un réel manque de confiance.

Italian: Nota dell'autore.
Mi è piaciuto molto scrivere la storia "La chiave". Infatti mi sono ispirato al racconto 'Le Veston' di Dino Buzzati. Quando ho iniziato a scriverlo ero ansioso, nervoso, titubante e sentivo una vera mancanza di fiducia.

Romanian: Nota autorului.

Romanian: Mi-a plăcut foarte mult să scriu povestea „Cheia". De fapt, m-am inspirat din povestea „Le Veston" a lui Dino Buzzati. Când am început să-l scriu, eram anxios, nervos, ezitant și simțeam o adevărată lipsă de încredere.

Spanish: Nota del autor.

Disfruté mucho escribiendo la historia "La llave". De hecho, me inspiré en el cuento 'Le Veston' de Dino Buzzati. Cuando comencé a escribirlo, estaba ansiosa, nerviosa, vacilante y sentía una verdadera falta de confianza.

Chinese - 中文：为您选择的语言或创意文本留出空间。

Then, like magic, the idea 'Key' appeared in my mind, and from that moment I had great strength in the belly area which gave me great enthusiasm. Then I began with delight and calm to write the story, in French, with great confidence. I felt a powerful and irrepressible force in my stomach. I could see, with my mind's eye, a glowing white ball of translucent light in my stomach area!

French: Puis, comme par magie, l'idée 'Clé' est apparue dans mon esprit, et à partir de ce moment j'ai eu une grande force dans la région du ventre qui m'a donné un grand enthousiasme. Puis j'ai commencé avec délice et calme à écrire l'histoire, en français, avec une grande assurance. J'ai senti une force puissante et irrépressible dans mon estomac. Je pouvais voir avec mon esprit une boule blanche brillante de lumière translucide dans la région de mon estomac!

Italian: Poi, come per magia, mi è venuta in mente l'idea 'Chiave', e da quel momento ho avuto una grande forza nella zona della pancia che mi ha dato grande entusiasmo. Poi ho iniziato con gioia e calma a scrivere la storia, in francese, con grande sicurezza. Ho sentito una forza potente e irrefrenabile nello stomaco. Potevo vedere con l'occhio della mia mente una sfera bianca brillante di luce traslucida nella zona del mio stomaco!

Romanian: Apoi, ca prin magie, mi-a apărut în minte ideea „Cheie", iar din acel moment am avut o mare forță în zona burticii care mi-a dat un mare entuziasm. Apoi am început cu încântare și calm să scriu povestea, în franceză, cu mare încredere. Am simțit o forță puternică și ireprimabilă în stomac. Am putut vedea cu ochii minții o minge albă strălucitoare de lumină translucidă în zona stomacului meu!

Spanish: Entonces, como por arte de magia, apareció en mi mente la idea 'Clave', y desde ese momento tuve una gran fuerza en la zona del vientre que me dio mucha ilusión. Entonces comencé con alegría y calma a escribir la historia, en francés, con mucha confianza. Sentí una fuerza poderosa e irreprimible en mi estómago. ¡Pude ver con el ojo de mi mente una bola blanca brillante de luz translúcida en el área de mi estómago!

Hindi: - हिंदी: अपनी पसंद की भाषा या रचनात्मक पाठ के लिए जगह।

When the story was finished, I was invited to read it aloud for the French class. As soon as I opened my mouth to speak the force, a ball of light rose very slowly from my belly area to go up and out of my mouth. This ball of white light stayed in front of my face in a powerful light, the size and shape of a volleyball. Whilst about 3% of the ball of light remained attached to the wall, or region, of my stomach.

French: Une fois l'histoire terminée, j'ai été invité à la lire à haute voix pour la classe de français. Dès que j'ai ouvert la bouche pour dire la force, une boule de lumière s'est élevée très lentement de la région de mon ventre pour monter et sortir de ma bouche. Cette boule de lumière blanche est restée devant mon visage dans une lumière puissante, de la taille et de la forme d'un ballon de volley. Tandis qu'environ 3% de la boule de lumière restait attachée à la paroi, ou région, de mon estomac.

Italian: Quando la storia fu finita fui invitato a leggerla ad alta voce per la classe di francese. Non appena ho aperto la bocca per pronunciare la forza, una sfera di luce si è alzata molto lentamente dalla zona del mio ventre per salire e uscire dalla mia bocca. Questa palla di luce bianca è rimasta davanti al mio viso in una luce potente, delle dimensioni e della forma di una palla da pallavolo. Mentre circa il 3% della sfera di luce è rimasto attaccato al muro, o regione, del mio stomaco.

Romanian: Când povestea s-a terminat, am fost invitat să o citesc cu voce tare pentru clasa de franceză. De îndată ce mi-am deschis gura pentru a spune forța, o minge de lumină s-a ridicat foarte încet din zona burții mele pentru a urca și a ieși din gură. Această minge de lumină albă a rămas în fața feței mele într-o lumină puternică, de mărimea și forma unei mingi de volei. În timp ce aproximativ 3% din bila de lumină a rămas atașată de peretele sau regiunea stomacului meu.

Spanish: Cuando terminó la historia, me invitaron a leerla en voz alta para la clase de francés. Tan pronto como abrí la boca para pronunciar la fuerza, una bola de luz se elevó muy lentamente desde el área de mi vientre para subir y salir de mi boca. Esta bola de luz blanca permaneció frente a mi cara en una luz poderosa, del tamaño y forma de una pelota de voleibol. Mientras que alrededor del 3% de la bola de luz permaneció adherida a la pared, o región, de mi estómago.

English: space for the language or creative text of your choice.

Afterward, this light completely invaded me, it was absorbed into my body and left me full of enthusiasm, energy, and clarity.

French: Par la suite, cette lumière m'a complètement envahie, elle a été absorbée dans mon corps et m'a laissé plein d'enthousiasme, d'énergie et de clarté.

Italian: In seguito, questa luce mi ha completamente invaso, è stata assorbita nel mio corpo e mi ha lasciato pieno di entusiasmo, energia e lucidità.

Romanian: După aceea, această lumină m-a invadat complet, a fost absorbită în corpul meu și m-a lăsat plin de entuziasm, energie și claritate.

Spanish: Después, esta luz me invadió por completo, se absorbió en mi cuerpo y me dejó lleno de entusiasmo, energía y claridad.

Français: espace pour la langue ou le texte créatif de votre choix.

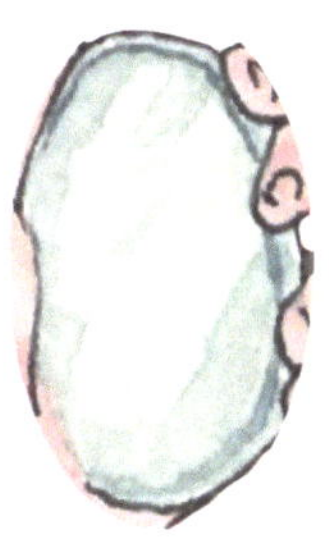

This proves that the fantastic really can burst into our lives and into the spiritual and invisible dimension when we least expect it.

French: Cela prouve que le fantastique peut vraiment faire irruption dans nos vies et dans la dimension spirituelle et invisible quand on s'y attend le moins.

Italian: Questo dimostra che il fantastico può davvero irrompere nella nostra vita e nella dimensione spirituale e invisibile quando meno ce lo aspettiamo.

Romanian: Acest lucru demonstrează că fantasticul poate izbucni într-adevăr în viețile noastre și în dimensiunea spirituală și invizibilă atunci când ne așteptăm mai puțin.

Spanish: Esto prueba que lo fantástico realmente puede irrumpir en nuestras vidas y en la dimensión espiritual e invisible cuando menos lo esperamos.

Italiano: spazio alla lingua o al testo creativo di tua scelta.

22 May 2022: Homestretch...

After collecting my key from the pawn shop I made my way to the cemetery by pushbike. It was a long cycle ride but that autumn day was fairly warm good weather.

French: 22 mai 2022: Dernière ligne droite...

Après avoir récupéré ma clé au prêteur sur gages, je me suis rendu au cimetière en vélo. C'était une longue balade à vélo, mais ce jour d'automne était un beau temps assez chaud.

Italian: 22 maggio 2022: Dirittura d'arrivo...

Dopo aver ritirato la mia chiave dal banco dei pegni, mi sono diretto al cimitero in bici. È stata una lunga corsa in bicicletta, ma quel giorno d'autunno era abbastanza caldo e bel tempo.

Romanian: 22 mai 2022: Acasa...

După ce mi-am luat cheia de la casa de amanet, m-am îndreptat spre cimitir cu pushbike. A fost o plimbare lungă cu bicicleta, dar ziua aceea de toamnă a fost vreme bună destul de caldă.

Spanish: 22 de mayo de 2022: La recta final...
Después de recoger mi llave de la casa de empeño, me dirigí al cementerio en una bicicleta de mano. Fue un largo paseo en bicicleta, pero ese día de otoño hacía buen tiempo bastante cálido.

Română: Spațiu pentru limba sau textul creativ la alegere.

The leaves were beginning to fall as it was late September. I felt at peace with the world. I had learnt over the years that the key could open any door including computer passwords, very useful if I forgot the password. But I learnt also to only use the key where I had a lawful right to enter or things may turn out badly.

French: Les feuilles commençaient à tomber car c'était fin septembre. Je me sentais en paix avec le monde. J'avais appris au fil des ans que la clé pouvait ouvrir n'importe quelle porte, y compris les mots de passe informatiques, très utile si j'oubliais le mot de passe. Mais j'ai aussi appris à n'utiliser la clé que là où j'avais le droit légitime d'entrer, sinon les choses pourraient mal tourner.

Italian: Le foglie cominciavano a cadere perché era fine settembre. Mi sentivo in pace con il mondo. Avevo imparato negli anni che la chiave poteva aprire qualsiasi porta comprese le password del computer, molto utile se dimenticavo la password. Ma ho anche imparato a usare la chiave solo dove avevo il legittimo diritto di entrare o le cose potevano andare male.

Romanian: Frunzele începeau să cadă la sfârșitul lunii septembrie. M-am simțit în pace cu lumea. Învățasem de-a lungul anilor că cheia poate deschide orice ușă inclusiv parolele computerului, foarte util dacă uitam parola. Dar am învățat, de asemenea, să folosesc cheia doar acolo unde aveam dreptul legal de a intra sau lucrurile pot merge prost.

Spanish: Las hojas comenzaban a caer ya que era finales de septiembre. Me sentí en paz con el mundo. A lo largo de los años había aprendido que la llave podía abrir cualquier puerta, incluidas las contraseñas de la computadora, muy útil si olvidaba la contraseña. Pero también aprendí a usar la llave solo donde tenía derecho legal a entrar o las cosas pueden salir mal.

Español: espacio para el idioma o texto creativo de su elección.

So, I kept the key for personal use only. I also learnt that the key was useful in unlocking mysteries but only at the right time. So, using qualities such as care, patience, humility, understanding, love, hope and charity actually prepared the way ahead and then one could find where the key would best go to unlock mysteries.

French: J'ai donc gardé la clé pour un usage personnel uniquement. J'ai aussi appris que la clé était utile pour débloquer des mystères mais seulement au bon moment. Ainsi, l'utilisation de qualités telles que l'attention, la patience, l'humilité, la compréhension, l'amour, l'espoir et la charité a en fait préparé la voie à suivre et on pourrait alors trouver où la clé irait le mieux pour déverrouiller les mystères.

Italian: Alora ho guardato la chiave solo per il uso personale. Ho anche capito che il disco era utile per sbloccare i misteri, ma solo nel momento giusto. Quindi, l'uso di qualita come la cura, la pazienza, l'umilta, la comprensione, l'amore, la speranza e la carita in realta prepararon il cammino a seguir e poi uno potra incontrare dove e ira migliore la chiave per desbloquear los misterios.

Romanian: Așa că am păstrat cheia doar pentru uz personal. Am mai învățat că cheia a fost utilă în deblocarea misterelor, dar numai la momentul potrivit. Așadar, folosirea calităților precum grija, răbdarea, smerenia, înțelegerea, dragostea, speranța și caritatea a pregătit de fapt calea de urmat și apoi s-ar putea găsi unde ar merge cel mai bine cheia pentru a dezvălui misterele.

Spanish: Así que guardé la llave solo para uso personal. También aprendí que la llave era útil para desbloquear misterios pero solo en el momento adecuado. Entonces, el uso de cualidades como el cuidado, la paciencia, la humildad, la comprensión, el amor, la esperanza y la caridad en realidad prepararon el camino a seguir y luego uno podría encontrar dónde iría mejor la clave para desbloquear los misterios.

Deutsch: Platz für die sprache oder den kreativen text ihrer wahl.

The key was helping me to develop my own potential, not for chasing a career or hoarding wealth but developing my own mind and using my own resources and spiritual connections to unlock the real me; rather than just living the roles needed to live in today's society.

French: La clé m'a aidé à développer mon propre potentiel, non pas pour poursuivre une carrière ou accumuler des richesses, mais pour développer mon propre esprit et utiliser mes propres ressources pour libérer le vrai moi; plutôt que de simplement vivre les rôles nécessaires pour vivre dans la société d'aujourd'hui.

Italian: La chiave è stata aiutarmi a sviluppare il mio potenziale, non per inseguire una carriera o accumulare ricchezze, ma sviluppare la mia mente e usare le mie risorse e connessioni spirituali per sbloccare il vero me; piuttosto che limitarsi a vivere i ruoli necessari per vivere nella società odierna.

Romanian: Cheia a fost să mă ajute să-mi dezvolt propriul potențial, nu pentru a urmări o carieră sau pentru a acumula avere, ci pentru a-mi dezvolta propria minte și pentru a-mi folosi propriile resurse și conexiuni spirituale pentru a debloca adevăratul eu; mai degrabă decât să trăiască doar rolurile necesare pentru a trăi în societatea actuală.

Spanish: La clave fue ayudarme a desarrollar mi propio potencial, no para perseguir una carrera o acumular riqueza, sino para desarrollar mi propia mente y usar mis propios recursos y conexiones espirituales para desbloquear mi verdadero yo; en lugar de simplemente vivir los roles necesarios para vivir en la sociedad actual.

Russian - Русский: пространство для языка или творческого текста по вашему выбору.

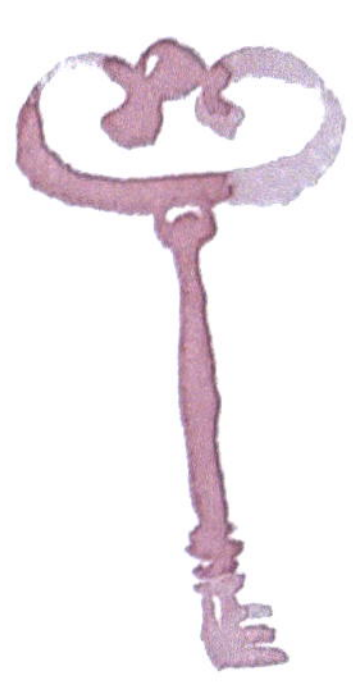

I arrived at the cemetery, the gate was open, I'd checked the opening times before I set off. I pushed my bike to the middle of the cemetery. Near to the door of the tomb was a bench so I sat down to take a break. I drank some water and ate a sandwich.

French: Je suis arrivé au cimetière, le portail était ouvert, j'avais vérifié les horaires d'ouverture avant de partir. J'ai poussé mon vélo jusqu'au milieu du cimetière. Près de la porte de la tombe se trouvait un banc, alors je me suis assis pour faire une pause. J'ai bu de l'eau et mangé un sandwich.

Italian: Sono arrivato al cimitero, il cancello era aperto, avevo controllato gli orari di apertura prima di partire. Ho spinto la mia bici in mezzo al cimitero. Vicino alla porta della tomba c'era una panca così mi sono seduto per fare una pausa. Ho bevuto un po' d'acqua e ho mangiato un panino.

Romanian: Am ajuns la cimitir, poarta era deschisă, am verificat orele de deschidere înainte de a pleca. Mi-am împins bicicleta până în mijlocul cimitirului. Lângă ușa mormântului era o bancă, așa că m-am așezat să iau o pauză. Am băut niște apă și am mâncat un sandviș.

Spanish: Llegué al cementerio, la puerta estaba abierta, comprobé los horarios de apertura antes de partir. Empujé mi bicicleta hasta el centro del cementerio. Cerca de la puerta de la tumba había un banco, así que me senté para tomar un descanso. Bebí un poco de agua y comí un sándwich.

Japonais - 日本語:選択した言語またはクリエイティブテキストのためのスペース。

I was in no hurry to open the door and I sat down meditating, or rather just letting my mind relax and controlling my breathing. I used a technique called 'the cool tongue meditation' that has its origins in Singapore. At the back of my mind were notions about human purpose, my personal purpose and mysteries surrounding the meaning of life and the hereafter.

French: Je n'étais pas pressé d'ouvrir la porte et je me suis assis en méditant, ou plutôt en laissant mon esprit se détendre et en contrôlant ma respiration. J'ai utilisé une technique appelée 'la méditation de la langue fraîche' qui a ses origines à Singapour. Au fond de mon esprit se trouvaient des notions sur le but humain, mon but personnel et les mystères entourant le sens de la vie et l'au-delà.

Italian: Non avevo fretta di aprire la porta e mi sono seduta a meditare, o meglio a rilassare la mente ea controllare il respiro. Ho usato una tecnica chiamata "la meditazione della lingua fredda" che ha le sue origini a Singapore. Nella parte posteriore della mia mente c'erano nozioni sullo scopo umano, il mio scopo personale e i misteri che circondavano il significato della vita e dell'aldilà.

Romanian: Nu mă grăbeam să deschid ușa și m-am așezat meditand, sau mai bine zis, lăsându-mi mintea să se relaxeze și controlându-mi respirația. Am folosit o tehnică numită „meditația cu limba rece" care își are originile în Singapore. În fundul minții mele erau noțiuni despre scopul uman, scopul meu personal și misterele care înconjoară sensul vieții și al viitorului.

Spanish: No tenía prisa por abrir la puerta y me senté a meditar, o más bien dejar que mi mente se relajara y controlara mi respiración. Utilicé una técnica llamada "la meditación de la lengua fría" que tiene su origen en Singapur. En el fondo de mi mente había nociones sobre el propósito humano, mi propósito personal y los misterios que rodean el significado de la vida y el más allá.

Svenska: Utrymme för det språk eller den kreativa text du väljer.

Did I really want to open that door today? I asked myself, was I ready to discover its hidden treasures?

French: Est-ce que je voulais vraiment ouvrir cette porte aujourd'hui? Je me suis demandé, étais-je prêt à découvrir ses trésors cachés?

Italian: Volevo davvero aprire quella porta oggi? Mi sono chiesto, ero pronto a scoprire i suoi tesori nascosti?

Romanian: Chiar am vrut să deschid acea ușă astăzi? M-am întrebat, eram gata să-i descopăr comorile ascunse?

Spanish: ¿Realmente quería abrir esa puerta hoy? Me pregunté, ¿estaba listo para descubrir sus tesoros escondidos? *64*

Chinese - 中文：为您选择的语言或创意文本留出空间。

As I sat and relaxed, I glanced at the door, and suddenly there was a two-inch ball of light in front of the door - was that the door keeper? It seemed to me like a fairy ball of clear, colourless, transparent light. It was about four feet off the ground, and then started slowly floating towards me, it felt magical and I was awed in the silence of its magic.

French: Alors que je m'asseyais et que je me détendais, j'ai jeté un coup d'œil à la porte, et soudain il y avait une boule de lumière de deux pouces devant la porte - était-ce le portier ? Cela m'apparaissait comme une boule féerique de lumière claire, incolore et transparente. Elle était à environ quatre pieds du sol, puis a commencé à flotter lentement vers moi, c'était magique et j'étais émerveillé par le silence de sa beauté.

Italian: Mentre mi sedevo e mi rilassavo, diedi un'occhiata alla porta e all'improvviso c'era una sfera di luce di due pollici davanti alla porta: era quello il custode? Mi sembrava una palla fatata di luce chiara, incolore, trasparente. Era a circa quattro piedi da terra e iniziò a fluttuare lentamente verso di me, sembrava magico e rimasi sbalordito nel silenzio della sua magia.

Romaian: În timp ce m-am așezat și m-am relaxat, m-am uitat la ușă și, deodată, în fața ușii a apărut o minge de lumină de doi centimetri - acela era portarul? Mi s-a părut o minge de zâne de lumină clară, incoloră, transparentă. Era la vreo patru picioare de sol și a început să plutească încet spre mine, sa simțit magic și am fost uimit de tăcerea magiei sale.

Spanish: Mientras me sentaba y me relajaba miré hacia la puerta, y de repente había una bola de luz de dos pulgadas frente a la puerta. ¿Era ese el portero? Me pareció como una bola de hadas de luz clara, incolora y transparente. Estaba a unos cuatro pies del suelo, y comenzó a flotar lentamente hacia mí, se sentía mágico y me asombró el silencio de su magia.

Hindi: हिंदी: अपनी पसंद की भाषा या रचनात्मक पाठ के लिए जगह।

The door was about four metres in front of me and the ball magically hovered to about four feet in front of me at about the distance of my aura. In the centre of that bubble of light was a pinprick of intense electric blue light. It then circled around me keeping the same distance, just at the edge of my aura.

French: La porte était à environ quatre mètres devant moi et la balle a plané comme par magie à environ quatre pieds devant moi à peu près à la distance de mon aura. Au centre de cette bulle de lumière se trouvait une piqûre d'épingle de lumière bleu électrique intense. Il a ensuite tourné autour de moi en gardant la même distance, juste au bord de mon aura.

Italian: La porta era a circa quattro metri davanti a me e la palla si librava magicamente a circa quattro piedi davanti a me, all'incirca alla distanza della mia aura. Al centro di quella bolla di luce c'era una puntina di intensa luce blu elettrico. Poi ha girato intorno a me mantenendo la stessa distanza, proprio al limite della mia aura.

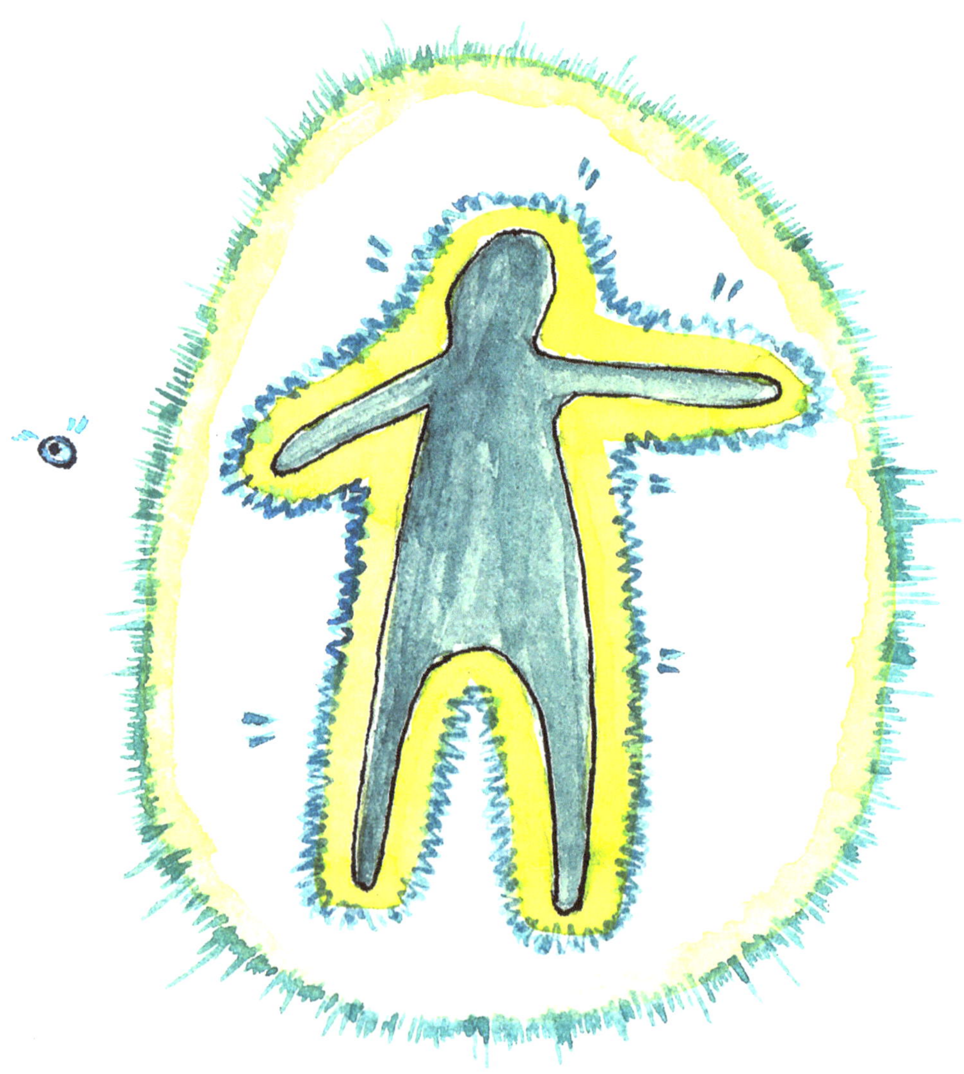

Romanian: Ușa era la aproximativ patru metri în fața mea și mingea a plutit în mod magic până la aproximativ patru picioare în fața mea, la aproximativ distanța de aura mea. În centrul acelei bule de lumină se afla o înțepătură de lumină albastră electrică intensă. Apoi sa rotit în jurul meu păstrând aceeași distanță, chiar la marginea aurei mele.

Spanish: La puerta estaba a unos cuatro metros frente a mí y la pelota flotaba mágicamente a unos cuatro pies frente a mí aproximadamente a la distancia de mi aura. En el centro de esa burbuja de luz había un pinchazo de intensa luz azul eléctrica. Luego dio vueltas a mi alrededor manteniendo la misma distancia, justo en el borde de mi aura.

English: space for the language or creative text of your choice.

It was a delightful and inspiring moment, then it slowly returned to where I first saw it and disappeared. I was left with a wonderful feeling of well-being and that all was going according to some divine plan! I simply felt spiritually uplifted and with a sense of oneness with all things wondrous.

French: Ce fut un moment délicieux et inspirant, puis il est lentement revenu là où je l'avais vu pour la première fois et a disparu. Il me restait une merveilleuse sensation de bien-être et que tout se déroulait selon un plan divin ! Je me sentais simplement, spirituellement élevé et avec un sentiment d'unité avec toutes les choses merveilleuses.

Italian: È stato un momento delizioso e stimolante, poi è tornato lentamente dove l'avevo visto per la prima volta ed è scomparso. Mi è rimasta una meravigliosa sensazione di benessere e che tutto stava andando secondo un piano divino! Mi sono semplicemente sentito spiritualmente sollevato e con un senso di unità con tutte le cose meravigliose.

Romanian: A fost un moment încântător și inspirator, apoi s-a întors încet acolo unde l-am văzut prima dată și a dispărut. Am rămas cu o minunată senzație de bine și că totul mergea după un plan divin! Pur și simplu m-am simțit înălțat spiritual și cu un sentiment de unitate cu toate lucrurile minunate.

Spanish: Fue un momento delicioso e inspirador, luego volvió lentamente a donde lo vi por primera vez y desapareció. ¡Me quedé con una maravillosa sensación de bienestar y de que todo iba de acuerdo con un plan divino! Simplemente me sentí espiritualmente elevado y con un sentido de unidad con todas las cosas maravillosas.

Français: espace pour la langue ou le texte créatif de votre choix.

The whole experience was uplifting. I remained sitting for about an hour more then I felt I had had enough for one day so grabbed my bike and made my way back home the mystery of the tomb could wait for another day.

French: Toute l'expérience a été édifiante. Je suis resté assis pendant environ une heure de plus, puis j'ai senti que j'en avais assez pour une journée, alors j'ai attrapé mon vélo et je suis rentré chez moi, le mystère de la tombe pouvait attendre un autre jour.

Italian: L'intera esperienza è stata edificante. Sono rimasto seduto per circa un'ora in più, poi ho sentito di averne avuto abbastanza per un giorno, quindi ho preso la bicicletta e sono tornato a casa, il mistero della tomba poteva aspettare un altro giorno.

Romanian: Întreaga experiență a fost înălțătoare. Am rămas așezat încă o oră, apoi am simțit că aveam destul pentru o zi, așa că mi-am luat bicicleta și m-am întors acasă, misterul mormântului ar putea aștepta o altă zi.

Spanish: Toda la experiencia fue edificante. Permanecí sentado durante aproximadamente una hora más, luego sentí que había tenido suficiente por un día, así que agarré mi bicicleta y regresé a casa, el misterio de la tumba podía esperar hasta otro día.

Italiano: spazio alla lingua o al testo creativo di tua scelta.

I felt elated as I returned to the city knowing in my heart that the riches of this world were not to be found behind some door or in a role pursuing a career, but rather found within oneself, alive in the real self and by attracting those magic moments to oneself.

French: Je me suis senti exalté en rentrant dans la ville en sachant dans mon cœur que les richesses de ce monde ne se trouvaient pas derrière une porte ou dans un rôle poursuivant une carrière, mais plutôt en soi, vivant dans le vrai soi et en attirant ces instants magiques pour soi.

Italian: Mi sono sentito euforico mentre tornavo in città sapendo nel mio cuore che le ricchezze di questo mondo non si trovavano dietro qualche porta o in un ruolo che perseguiva una carriera, ma piuttosto dentro di sé, vive nel vero sé e attirando coloro momenti magici per se stessi.

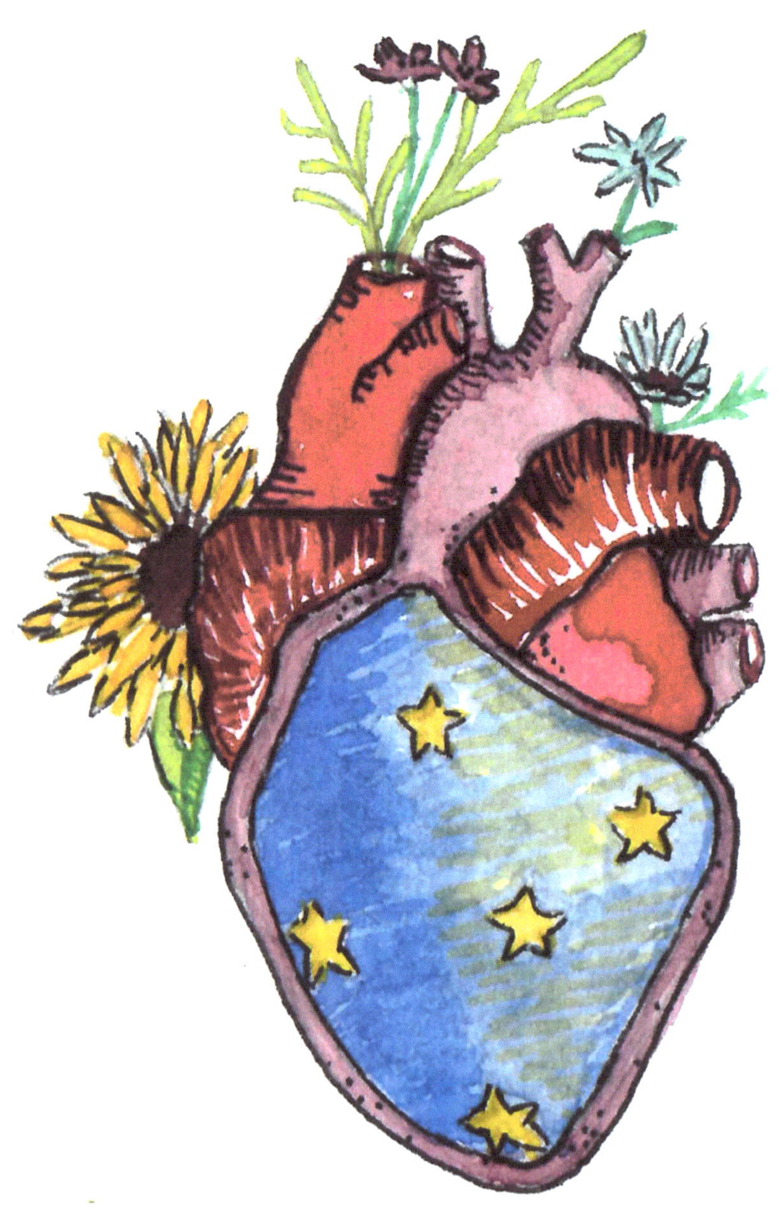

Romanian: M-am simțit bucuros când m-am întors în oraș știind în inima mea că bogățiile acestei lumi nu se găsesc în spatele vreunei uși sau într-un rol care urmărește o carieră, ci mai degrabă se găsesc în interiorul tău, viu în eul real și atragând acele momente magice pentru sine.

Spanish: Me sentí eufórico cuando regresé a la ciudad sabiendo en mi corazón que las riquezas de este mundo no se encontraban detrás de una puerta o en un rol que perseguía una carrera, sino que se encontraban dentro de uno mismo, vivo en el yo real y atrayendo esos momentos mágicos para uno mismo.

Română: Spațiu pentru limba sau textul creativ la alegere.

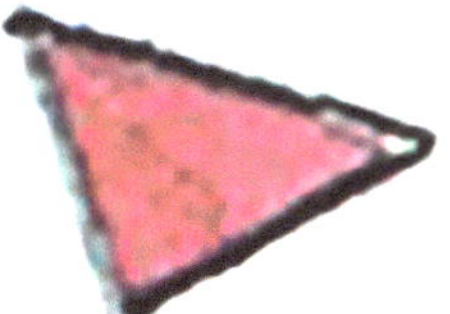

El fin

Fine

La fin!

Sfârșitul

Español: espacio para el idioma o texto creativo de su elección.

Author David Gordon Stanley

Auteur David Gordon Stanley

Aide translation Lorelei Surdu for Simona

Aide à la traduction Lorelei Surdu for Simona

Illustrated by Dimitra Megkou

Illustré par Dimitra Megkou

About 14,000 words in total.

With about 3,600 English words translated into French, Spanish, Italian and Romanian.

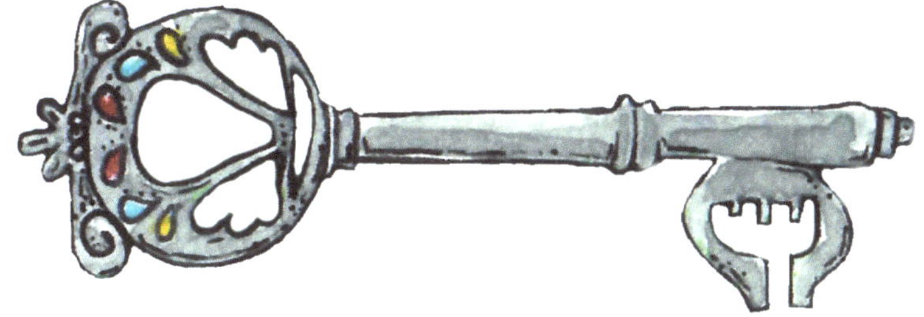 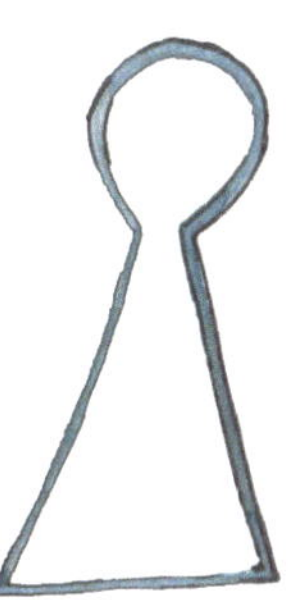

Deutsch: Platz für die sprache oder den kreativen text ihrer wahl.

i

Interactive suggestion page:

There are spaces at the bottom of each page and at the back of the book to either add a self chosen 3rd language or create one's own text that may be inspired by the designs and existing text.

Text can be added to pages either by penciling in a translation or creating and purchasing your own online stickers of the text and designs required.

Online Google translate can be used to give a basic translation of the text in the book, but it is advised to ask a language translator to confirm any online translation.

Please note:
• Before penciling in the book write the text on a blank piece of paper.
• When using stickers take care to place the sticker as required!
• For more information and ideas about stickers etc. please go online to the The Key suggestion page - link below:

- https://sites.google.com/view/the-key-la-cle/suggestion-page

Examples of translation and creative texts are given below.

Page 1. 3rd Language Choice – Español

Era un hermoso día de verano, los pájaros cantaban en los árboles y el aire era refrescante. Estaba caminando por la ciudad y tomé un atajo por el cementerio.

Swedish: Det var en vacker sommardag, fåglarna sjöng i träden och luften var uppfriskande. Jag gick genom staden och tog en genväg genom kyrkogården.

Or a creative text:

 Postscript creative in English:

The next day was also very warm and sunny, could this be the start of an Indian summer? I was sat on a bench in the local park taking shade under my sombrero, and feeding a few wood pigeons with the leftover crumbs of a cheese sandwich. On my right was an oak tree where on a branch, from the corner of my eye, I could see a bushy-tailed squirrel. It was looking around twitching whilst appearing to ignore me completely. At the same time, I was meditating on a few philosophic mysteries where I'd needed a key. I was dwelling on the Ancient Astronomical Clock in Prague and mulling over its connection to the pineal gland and the dark side of the Sun!

i.i

Interactive suggestion page:

Postscript Creative French:

Le lendemain était aussi très chaud et ensoleillé, pourrait-ce être le début d'un été indien ?
J'étais assis sur un banc dans le parc local prenant l'ombre sous mon sombrero, et nourrissant
quelques pigeons de bois avec les restes de miettes d'un sandwich au fromage.

À ma droite, il y avait un chêne où, sur une branche, je pouvais voir un écureuil à queue touffue,
du coin de l'œil. Il regardait autour de lui en faisant semblant de m'ignorer complètement.

En même temps, je méditais sur quelques mystères philosophiques où j'avais besoin d'une clé.
J'ai ruminé sur l'Ancienne Horloge Astronomique à Prague et réfléchissant sur sa connexion
avec la glande pinéale et le côté sombre du Soleil!

Postscript Italian:

Anche il giorno successivo era molto caldo e soleggiato, potrebbe essere l'inizio di un'estate
indiana?
Ero seduto su una panchina nel parco locale a prendere l'ombra sotto il mio sombrero e a
dare da mangiare ad alcuni colombacci con le briciole avanzate di un panino al formaggio.
Alla mia destra c'era una quercia dove su un ramo potevo vedere uno scoiattolo dalla coda
folta, con la coda dell'occhio. Si guardava intorno contraendosi mentre sembrava ignorarmi
completamente. Allo stesso tempo, meditavo su alcuni misteri filosofici per i quali avrei avuto
bisogno di una chiave. Mi soffermavo sull'Antico Orologio Astronomico di Praga e rimuginavo
sulla sua connessione con la ghiandola pineale e il lato oscuro del Sole!

Postscript Romanian:

A doua zi a fost, de asemenea, foarte caldă și însorită, ar putea fi acesta începutul unei veri
indiene?
Eram așezat pe o bancă în parcul local, luând umbră sub sombrero-ul meu și hrănind câțiva
porumbei de pădure cu firimiturile rămase dintr-un sandviș cu brânză. În dreapta mea era un
stejar unde pe o creangă vedeam cu coada ochiului o veveriță cu coadă stufoasă. Se uita în
jur zvâcnind în timp ce părea să mă ignore complet.
În același timp, meditam la câteva mistere filozofice în care aș avea nevoie de o cheie. Locuiam
pe Ceasul Astronomic Antic din Praga și mă gândeam la legătura lui cu glanda pineală și cu
partea întunecată a Soarelui!

Posdata creativa en español:

El día siguiente también fue muy cálido y soleado, ¿podría ser este el comienzo de un verano indio?

Estaba sentado en un banco del parque local tomando sombra bajo mi sombrero y alimentando a unos cuantos palomas torcaces con las migas sobrantes de un sándwich de queso. A mi derecha había un roble donde en una rama, por el rabillo del ojo, pude ver una ardilla de cola tupida. Fue mirando a su alrededor retorciéndose mientras parece ignorarme por completo. Al mismo tiempo, yo estaba meditando sobre algunos misterios filosóficos donde necesitaba una clave. Estaba pensando en el Antiguo Reloj Astronómico en Praga y reflexionando sobre su conexión con la glándula pineal y ¡El lado oscuro del sol!

i.ii

Prague clock!

ii

Page de suggestion:

Il y a des espaces au bas de chaque page et à la fin du livre pour :

- soit ajouter une 3e langue choisie que l'on choisie soi-même,
- soit créer son propre texte qui peut être inspiré par les dessins et/ou le texte existant.

 Le texte peut être rajouté aux pages soit en l'écrivant, soit en commandant en ligne des autocollants avec le texte ou les motifs requis.

Google Translate peut être utilisé pour donner une traduction de base du texte du livre, mais il est conseillé de demander à un traducteur de confirmer toute traduction en ligne.

Pour plus d'informations et d'idées sur les autocollants, veuillez vous rendre sur le lien de la page de suggestion du livre « la clé »

- https://sites.google.com/view/the-key-la-cle/suggestion-page

Notes:
1.   Avant d'écrire dans le livre, notez le texte sur une feuille vierge.
2.   Lorsque vous utilisez des autocollants, veuillez placer l'autocollant comme il faut!

Des exemples de traductions et de textes créatifs sont donnés ci-dessous.
Traductions Page 1. Alegerea a 3-a Limba Română:

Era o zi frumoasă de vară, păsările cântau în copaci și aerul era răcoritor. Mergeam prin oraș și am luat o scurtătură prin cimitir.

Chinese: Page 1. 第三選擇羅馬尼亞語
Dì sān xuǎnzé luómǎníyǎ yǔ
那是一個美麗的夏日，鳥兒在樹上歌唱，空氣清新。我正穿過城鎮，走近路穿過墓地。
Nà shì yīgè měilì de xià rì, niǎo er zài shù shàng gēchàng, kōngqì qīngxīn. Wǒ zhèng chuānguò chéngzhèn, zǒu jìn lù chuānguò mùdì.

Efterskriftskreativ på Svenska

Dagen efter var också väldigt varm och solig, kan detta vara starten på en indiansommar? Jag satt på en bänk i den lokala parken och tog skugga under min sombrero och matade några skogsduvor med resterna av en ostmacka. På min högra sida stod en ek där jag på en gren, från ögonvrån, kunde se en buskstjärtad ekorre. Den tittade runt och ryckte samtidigt som den såg ut att ignorera mig helt. Samtidigt mediterade jag över några filosofiska mysterier där jag hade behövt en nyckel. Jag höll på den antika astronomiska klockan i Prag och funderade över dess koppling till tallkottkörteln och solens mörka sida!

iii

World views:

English: These blank pages can be used to add a translated text of another language.

For more information go to the Key website:

https://sites.google.com/view/the-key-la-cle/home

French – Français: Ces pages vierges peuvent être utilisées pour ajouter un texte traduit d'une autre langue.

Italian - Italiano: Queste pagine vuote possono essere utilizzate per aggiungere un testo tradotto in un'altra lingua.

Romanian – Română: Aceste pagini goale pot fi folosite pentru a adăuga un text tradus într-o altă limbă.

Spanish - Español: Estas páginas en blanco se pueden usar para agregar un texto traducido de otro idioma.

Swedish – svenska: Dessa tomma sidor kan användas för att lägga till en översatt text från ett annat språk.

Japanese:

これらの空白ページを使用して、他の言語から翻訳されたテキストを追加できます。詳細については、「The Key 」の　　Web　サイトを参照してください。

Korera no kūhaku pēji o shiyō shite, hoka no gengo kara hon'yaku sa reta tekisuto o tsuika dekimasu. Shōsai ni tsuite wa,`The kī' no u~ebu saito o sanshō shite kudasai.

https://sites.google.com/view/the-key-la-cle/home

About the book

The Key -La Clé, is a young man's spiritual adventure of discovery & development, it includes some spiritual phenomena a true story blended into a fictional narrative. It is also an illustrated fairy tale for young children and teenagers. It is easy to read and can be used as an educational tool for those of any age serious about becoming bilingual or multilingual. It's written in English, French, Italian, Romanian and Spanish. Space is provided on each page to pencil in or place stickers for those who wish to include other languages or do their own artwork. Other languages in the book include, Russian, Chinese, Japanese, Swedish, German, and Hindi. The story is the beginning of an adventure to unlock hidden mysteries that could be useful to find and develop one's own true self.

About the author

After an accident that left me slightly handicapped at age 9, I developed a passion for finding the meaning of life. At age 17, with average school qualifications, I signed up for 22 years in the military, of which 4 years was active service. In the 80s, whilst working as a salesman, I developed my spiritual life with language skills, poetry, and arts. In 2009 after many years of teaching English to adults in France, my French was good enough to attempt taking a French DAEU Diploma. It was at that time that I wrote a rough copy of the story 'La Clé' in French. I was at the same time writing my autobiography which was confirmed to be also an independent autobiographical spiritual doctoral thesis. For further information go to - The Key website:
https://sites.google.com/view/the-key-la-cle/home

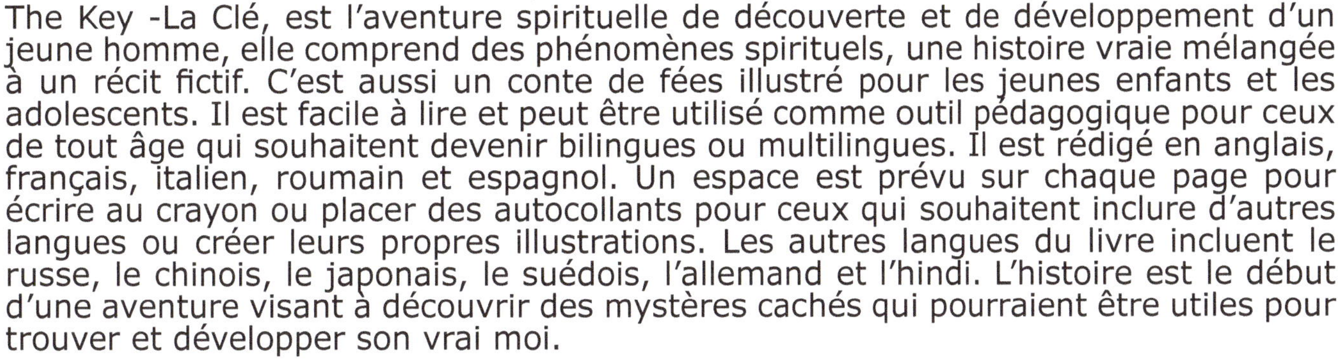

Français

À propos du livre

The Key -La Clé, est l'aventure spirituelle de découverte et de développement d'un jeune homme, elle comprend des phénomènes spirituels, une histoire vraie mélangée à un récit fictif. C'est aussi un conte de fées illustré pour les jeunes enfants et les adolescents. Il est facile à lire et peut être utilisé comme outil pédagogique pour ceux de tout âge qui souhaitent devenir bilingues ou multilingues. Il est rédigé en anglais, français, italien, roumain et espagnol. Un espace est prévu sur chaque page pour écrire au crayon ou placer des autocollants pour ceux qui souhaitent inclure d'autres langues ou créer leurs propres illustrations. Les autres langues du livre incluent le russe, le chinois, le japonais, le suédois, l'allemand et l'hindi. L'histoire est le début d'une aventure visant à découvrir des mystères cachés qui pourraient être utiles pour trouver et développer son vrai moi.

A propos de l'auteur

Après un accident qui m'a rendu légèrement handicapé à l'âge de 9 ans, j'ai développé une passion pour trouver le sens de la vie. A 17 ans, avec un niveau scolaire moyen, je m'engage pour 22 ans dans l'armée dont 4 ans de service actif. Dans les années 80, alors que je travaillais comme vendeur, j'ai développé ma vie spirituelle avec les compétences linguistiques, la poésie et les arts. En 2009, après de nombreuses années d'enseignement de l'anglais à des adultes en France, mon français était assez bon pour tenter de passer un diplôme français du DAEU. C'est à cette époque que j'ai écrit un brouillon de l'histoire 'La Clé' en français. J'étais en même temps en train d'écrire mon autobiographie qui a été confirmée comme étant aussi une thèse de doctorat spirituelle indépendante. Pour plus d'informations, rendez-vous sur le site Web de The Key: https://sites.google.com/view/the-key-la-cle/home

Italiano

A proposito del libro

The Key -La Clé, è l'avventura spirituale di scoperta e sviluppo di un giovane, include alcuni fenomeni spirituali, una storia vera mescolata a una narrativa immaginaria. È anche una fiaba illustrata per bambini e adolescenti. È facile da leggere e può essere utilizzato come strumento educativo per coloro di qualsiasi età che intendono diventare bilingue o multilingue. È scritto in inglese, francese, italiano, rumeno e spagnolo. Su ogni pagina è previsto spazio per scrivere a matita o posizionare adesivi per coloro che desiderano includere altre lingue o realizzare la propria opera d'arte. Altre lingue nel libro includono russo, cinese, giapponese, svedese, tedesco e hindi. La storia è l'inizio di un'avventura per svelare misteri nascosti che potrebbero essere utili per trovare e sviluppare il proprio vero sé.

Circa l'autore

Dopo un incidente che mi ha lasciato leggermente handicappato all'età di 9 anni, ho sviluppato la passione per trovare il senso della vita. A 17 anni, con titolo di studio medio, ho arruolato 22 anni nell'esercito, di cui 4 in servizio attivo. Negli anni '80, mentre lavoravo come venditore, ho sviluppato la mia vita spirituale con competenze linguistiche, poetiche e artistiche. Nel 2009, dopo molti anni di insegnamento dell'inglese ad adulti in Francia, il mio francese è stato abbastanza buono da tentare di prendere un diploma DAEU francese. Fu allora che scrissi una copia approssimativa del racconto 'La Clé' in francese. Nello stesso tempo stavo scrivendo la mia autobiografia che si è confermata anche una tesi di dottorato spirituale indipendente. Per ulteriori informazioni vai su - Il sito web di The Key: https://sites.google.com/view/the-key-la-cle/home

Română

Despre carte

Cheia - La Clé, este o aventură spirituală de descoperire și dezvoltare a unui tânăr, include unele fenomene spirituale, o poveste adevărată amestecată într-o narațiune fictivă. Este, de asemenea, un basm ilustrat pentru copii mici și adolescenți. Este ușor de citit și poate fi folosit ca instrument educațional pentru cei de orice vârstă care doresc să devină bilingvi sau multilingvi. Este scris în engleză, franceză, italiană, română și spaniolă. Pe fiecare pagină este oferit spațiu pentru a creiona sau a plasa autocolante pentru cei care doresc să includă alte limbi sau să-și facă propriile lucrări de artă. Alte limbi din carte includ rusă, chineză, japoneză, suedeză, germană și hindi. Povestea este începutul unei aventuri pentru a debloca misterele ascunse care ar putea fi utile pentru a găsi și dezvolta propriul sine adevărat.

Despre autor

După un accident care m-a lăsat ușor handicapat la vârsta de 9 ani, mi-am dezvoltat pasiunea pentru a găsi sensul vieții. La 17 ani, cu calificare școlară medie, m-am înscris pentru 22 de ani în armată, din care 4 ani în serviciu activ. În anii 80, în timp ce lucram ca vânzător, mi-am dezvoltat viața spirituală cu abilități lingvistice, poezie și arte. În 2009, după mulți ani în care am predat limba engleză pentru adulți în Franța, franceza mea a fost suficient de bună pentru a încerca să iau o diplomă franceză DAEU. În acel moment am scris o copie brută a poveștii „La Clé" în franceză. În același timp îmi scriam autobiografia, care a fost confirmată a fi și o teză de doctorat spirituală independentă. Pentru mai multe informații, accesați site-ul - The Key: https://sites.google.com/view/the-key-la-cle/home

Español

Acerca del libro

The Key -La Clé, es la aventura espiritual de descubrimiento y desarrollo de un joven e incluye algunos fenómenos espirituales una historia real mezclada con una narrativa ficticia. También es un cuento de hadas ilustrado para niños y adolescentes. Es fácil de leer y puede utilizarse como herramienta educativa para aquellos de cualquier edad interesados en la idea de llegar a ser bilingües o multilingües. Está escrito en inglés, francés, italiano, rumano y español. En cada página se proporciona un espacio para escribir con lápiz o colocar calcomanías, para aquellos que deseen incluir otros idiomas o crear sus propias obras de arte. Otros idiomas incluídos en el libro son ruso, chino, japonés, sueco, alemán e hindi. La historia es el comienzo de una aventura para desbloquear misterios ocultos que podría ser útil para encontrar y desarrollar su verdadero yo.

Sobre el Autor

Después de un accidente que me dejó levemente discapacitado a los 9 años, desarrollé una pasión por encontrar el sentido de la vida. A los 17 años, con calificaciones escolares promedio, me inscribí por 22 años en el ejército, de los cuales 4 años fueron de servicio activo. En los años 80, mientras trabajaba como vendedor, desarrollé mi vida espiritual con habilidades lingüísticas, poéticas y artísticas. En 2009, después de muchos años de enseñar inglés a adultos en Francia, mi francés era lo suficientemente bueno como para intentar obtener un diploma DAEU de francés. Fue entonces cuando escribí un borrador del cuento 'La Clé' en francés. Al mismo tiempo, estaba escribiendo mi autobiografía, que se confirmó que también era una tesis doctoral espiritual independiente. Para obtener más información, visite el sitio web de The Key: https://sites.google.com/view/the-key-la-cle/home

Hindi: हिंदी: अपनी पसंद की भाषा या रचनात्मक पाठ के लिए जगह।

The Key - La Clé, is a young man's spiritual adventure of discovery & development, it includes some spiritual phenomena a true story blended into a fictional narrative. It is also an illustrated fairy tale for children, teenagers, and adults. It is easy to read and can be used as an educational tool for those of any age serious about becoming bilingual or multilingual. It's written in English, French, Italian, Romanian and Spanish. Space is provided on each page to pencil in or place stickers for those who wish to include other languages or do their own artwork. Other languages in the book include, Russian, Chinese, Japanese, Swedish, German, and Hindi. The story is the beginning of an adventure to unlock hidden mysteries that could be useful to find and develop one's own true self.

About the Author: After an accident that left me slightly handicapped at age 9, I developed a passion for finding the meaning of life. At age 17, with average school qualifications, I signed up for 22 years in the military, of which 4 years was active service. In the 80s, whilst working as a salesman, I developed my spiritual life with language skills, poetry, and arts. In 2009 after many years of teaching English to adults in France, my French was good enough to attempt taking a French DAEU Diploma. It was at that time that I wrote a rough copy of the story 'La Clé' in French. I was at the same time writing my autobiography which was confirmed to be also an independent autobiographical spiritual doctoral thesis. For further information go to - The Key website: https://sites.google.com/view/the-key-la-cle/home

Author David Gordon Stanley
Auteur David Gordon Stanley

Aide translation Lorelei Surdu
Aide à la traduction Lorelei Surdu

Illustrated by Dimitra Megkou
Illustré par Dimitra Megkou

ISBN 000-0-0000-0000-0

WorkBook PRESS